A Ghos

Jessica and Elizabeth stood close to the window.

"Doesn't the bell tower look scary?" Jessica said.

The other Snoopers crowded around. "It's raining cats and dogs outside," Elizabeth said. It was very dark, too, except when the lightning lit up the sky.

Suddenly, everyone gasped. A figure in a long, hooded robe ran past the window and vanished around the corner of the tower!

"Did you see that?" Jessica asked. Her heart was pounding so loudly she could hear the *thump-thump-thump* in her ears.

"It was the monk's ghost!" Todd yelled.

Bantam Skylark Books in the SWEET VALLEY KIDS series

SWEET VALLEY KIDS
SUPER SNOOPER #3

THE CASE OF THE HAUNTED CAMP

Written by
Molly Mia Stewart

Created by
FRANCINE PASCAL

Illustrated by
Ying-Hwa Hu

A BANTAM SKYLARK BOOK ®
NEW YORK · TORONTO · LONDON · SYDNEY · AUCKLAND

RL 2, 005-008

THE CASE OF THE HAUNTED CAMP
A Bantam Skylark Book / June 1992

Sweet Valley High® and Sweet Valley Kids are trademarks
of Francine Pascal.

Conceived by Francine Pascal.

Produced by Daniel Weiss Associates, Inc.
33 West 17th Street
New York, NY 10011

Cover art by Susan Tang

Skylark Books is a registered trademark of Bantam Books,
a division of Bantam Doubleday Dell Publishing Group, Inc.
Registered in U.S. Patent and Trademark Office and elsewhere.

ISBN 0-553-15894-5

Published simultaneously in the United States and Canada

Bantam Books are published by Bantam Books, a division of Bantam Doubleday
Dell Publishing Group, Inc. Its trademark, consisting of the words "Bantam
Books" and the portrayal of a rooster, is Registered in U.S. Patent and Trademark
Office and in other countries. Marca Registrada. Bantam Books, 1540 Broadway,
New York, New York 10036.

PRINTED IN THE UNITED STATES OF AMERICA

CWO   10 9 8 7 6 5 4 3 2

To Alice Elizabeth Wenk

CHAPTER 1

Another Case to Solve

Jessica Wakefield opened the jar of orange paint and dipped her brush inside. *SPLAT*! The paint splashed against her clay pot. Paint dribbled onto the table. "I hate arts and crafts," Jessica grumbled. "Day camp is so boring."

"No, it's not," her twin sister, Elizabeth, said. "I love day camp. It's fun. We get to do so many different things. Besides, I love being a Porpoise." The Porpoises was the name of the seven-year-old group at camp.

Jessica made a face.

Jessica and Elizabeth were identical twins. They both had blue-green eyes and shoulder-length blond hair with bangs. Even though they looked the same on the outside, they were very different on the inside. Elizabeth liked all the games at Camp San Benito. She was good at archery and swimming and was learning how to tie complicated knots. Her favorite part of camp was the storytelling hour, when different counselors told funny or scary tales.

To Jessica, day camp meant being outside in the hot sun and getting messy. She hated soccer and kickball and carrying her damp bathing suit home every day. She liked being with her best friends, Lila Fowler and Ellen Riteman. But they couldn't play with their dolls or stuffed animals, even during rest hour.

As long as Elizabeth was there, though,

Jessica wasn't too unhappy. The twins were different in many ways, but they were best friends. Being twins meant they shared everything and did everything together.

"Don't forget about the camp-out," Amy Sutton said from across the arts and crafts table.

"I can't wait," Todd Wilkins said. "It's going to be cool."

Jessica nodded happily. "Finally something fun is going to happen."

"And Jennifer is really nice," Eva Simpson said. Jennifer was their group counselor. She was seventeen, and everyone liked her a lot.

Elizabeth smiled at Jessica. "See? There's lots to like about camp."

"Maybe," Jessica said. "But I wish something really exciting would happen."

"Do you mean like another mystery?" Winston Egbert asked.

"Yes!" Jessica said. "That's what we need. We could be the Snoopers again. We're all here."

The Snoopers was a mystery club. There were eight members: Elizabeth, Jessica, Todd, Winston, Amy, Eva, Lila, and Ellen. They were all in the same class at Sweet Valley Elementary School, and now they were in the same group at camp.

They had solved two mysteries together so far, and they were always looking for another one to solve. But mysteries were hard to find.

"I have an idea," Lila said. "We could find out if Jennifer has a boyfriend."

Todd and Winston made pretend gagging sounds. Elizabeth made a face, and Jessica giggled.

"That's not very mysterious," Amy pointed out. "You could just ask her if she has a boyfriend."

5

"I already did," Ellen said, waving her paintbrush in the air. "She won't tell me. She's being very mysterious about it."

Jessica leaned across the table. "We could follow her—"

"Shh! Here she comes," Lila whispered.

Jennifer walked over to the table where all the Snoopers were working on their clay pots. "We're going out to play kickball in five minutes," she said. "So please start putting your projects away."

"Kickball, yuck," Ellen muttered.

"Come on, hurry up," Winston said, jamming the caps back on the paint jars. He had green paint smears on his hands and his forehead.

Jessica wiped her part of the table with a sponge. She had orange paint on her hands, and she carefully checked her pink shorts and shirt to see if she had spilled any on them.

6

Soon, the whole group was out on the sports field. It was a long walk from the arts and crafts building. Next to the field was a high stone wall. Jessica walked over and stood in front of the wall. She hoped no one would kick the ball out that far. Every day they played a different sport, and Jessica was tired of it.

She leaned against the wall and looked up at the sky. It was getting dark and cloudy.

"What are you doing way out there?" Jennifer called.

"I'm playing outfield," Jessica said. "What's behind this wall?"

"That was a mission two hundred years ago. Monks used to live there. Now it's a museum. It's called San Benito, and that's why our camp is called Camp San Benito."

"Can we—" Jessica began.

Suddenly, there was a loud clap of thunder.

7

"Rain!" Jessica said. She felt a big raindrop plop onto her face.

"Let's go swimming," Winston shouted happily.

"Let's go inside," Jennifer called. She pointed to a gate in the wall. "Run into the museum. It's much closer."

Elizabeth ran over to Jessica and grabbed her hand. The rain was starting to come down hard. "Come on," Elizabeth said. "We're getting soaked."

"See," Jessica said as they started to run. "I told you day camp wasn't fun!"

CHAPTER 2

The Ghost Story

"Whew!" Elizabeth said, stopping under an arch. "It's pouring."

All the Porpoises were inside the museum courtyard. There were large stone pillars, archways all around, and a pretty fountain in the middle. Rain came down like a waterfall from the roof of the buildings. The thunder and lightning seemed as if they would never stop.

"That was a close call," Jennifer said, laughing. "Is everybody here? Let's have a buddy check."

Elizabeth took Jessica's hand. All the other kids in the group found their buddies and stood together. Elizabeth looked around the museum. It looked pretty.

Suddenly, a large wooden door opened and a tall man came out.

"Visitors!" he said. "Welcome to San Benito."

"We're from the day camp," Jennifer explained. "We came in to get out of the rain."

The man gave everyone a friendly smile. "I'm Mr. Sanchez, the museum director. Please come inside, campers."

Elizabeth was very curious about the museum. She hoped Jennifer would let them look around.

"How about it, gang?" Jennifer asked the group. "Should we take a look? Then we could have our story hour right here. Maybe

10

by then the rain will have ended and we can go back to camp."

Everyone looked out at the rain. Mr. Sanchez laughed. "It's definitely a day to stay indoors. Besides, I've got a good ghost story to tell you all."

"Ghost story?" Jessica whispered. She looked at her sister and shivered. "I hope it's really scary."

The Porpoises filed in through the wooden door. Elizabeth and Jessica and the rest of the Snoopers walked together in their own small group.

"This is kind of a creepy place," Ellen said softly.

"It seems normal to me," Winston said. "Like any old haunted house." Winston loved to clown around.

Mr. Sanchez stopped in the middle of the hallway, and the campers gathered around to

12

hear. The thunder sounded far away now that they were inside the thick stone walls.

"This mission used to be a very special kind of church," Mr. Sanchez explained. "It was a monastery. Who knows what that means?"

Elizabeth raised her hand. "A place where monks live."

"That's right," Mr. Sanchez said. "There aren't any monks here anymore, but there used to be a lot. They learned about religion and raised animals and grew crops and took care of the church."

"Tell us the ghost story," Ricky Capaldo called.

Mr. Sanchez put one finger to his lips. "Come this way, and I'll tell you."

"This is fun," Eva whispered.

"I hope we don't have to look at old stuff," Lila said. "I don't like museums. It's like being in school."

13

"It's better than school," Jessica said. "We don't have to take any tests."

Elizabeth liked the way their footsteps echoed on the stone floors. The hallway was long with a high ceiling. It was like being inside a tunnel. The group passed by a tiny, round window in the wall, and everyone could see that it was raining outside.

"This is where I'll tell you the ghost story," Mr. Sanchez said. He stopped beside a large window. Across another yard, they could see a tall tower.

"In the year 1790, some dangerous bandits came to a village nearby," Mr. Sanchez began. "A monk from San Benito knew they would be coming to Sweet Valley next, and he rushed back to the mission to warn everyone.

"Some of the desperados chased the monk back to the church. But he ran up to the bell tower and rang the bells to warn the town."

Mr. Sanchez paused and pointed to the tower outside the window. "When the bandits got to the top of the tower, the monk had disappeared."

Elizabeth gulped as she stared at the bell tower. A shiver went down her spine. She was happy the lights were on where they were standing.

"Now people say they sometimes see the ghost of that monk walking through the mission. And the legend goes that whenever trouble is coming, the monk will ring the bells." Mr. Sanchez let his voice drop down to a whisper.

Everyone was silent for a moment.

"Is that story true?" Todd asked.

"There's no such things as ghosts," Lila said.

"Do you think we'll hear the bells?" Jessica asked.

"Don't worry," Mr. Sanchez said with a smile. "The bells don't have any ringers inside of them now."

"It's just a story, group," Jennifer said. "Don't worry."

Just then, there was a huge *BA-BOOM-BOOM* of thunder. All the lights went out.

CHAPTER 3

The Monk's Ghost

Jessica screamed.

"What happened?" Ellen called out.

"Buddy up!" Jennifer yelled. "Take your buddy's hand."

Jessica felt Elizabeth take her hand in the dark. Lightning flashed outside the window.

"Don't be scared," Elizabeth whispered.

"I'm not scared," Jessica whispered back. "It's like being in a haunted house at a Halloween party. It's scary and fun at the same time."

"I can't find my buddy," Lila wailed.

"Jennifer! Make the lights go back on!" Amy said.

"Don't worry, everyone," Jennifer said above the loud voices. "The lights will be on in a minute."

Mr. Sanchez spoke up. "Just stay where you are, kids. I'll get some flashlights."

Jessica and Elizabeth stood close to the window. Each time the lightning flashed, they could see the other Snoopers. Ellen and Lila were standing together, Amy and Eva were holding hands, and Todd and Winston were making spooky ghost noises to scare each other.

"Do you think the ghost could be real?" Elizabeth asked quietly.

Amy made a creepy face and held her hands out to Eva. "Oooh-aaah," she moaned.

"Quit it," Eva said, giggling.

18

Jessica giggled, too. "Doesn't the bell tower look scary?" she asked. "Every time there's lightning, you can see it."

The Snoopers crowded around the window. "It's raining cats and dogs outside," Elizabeth said. She loved that expression. Grandpa Wakefield used it all the time. It meant it was raining very hard. It was very dark, too, except when the lightning lit up the sky.

Suddenly, everyone gasped. A figure in a long, hooded robe ran past the window and vanished around the corner of the tower.

"Did you see that?" Jessica said. Her heart was pounding so loudly she could hear the *thump-thump-thump* in her ears.

"It was the monk's ghost!" Todd yelled. "Cool!"

Everyone started yelling and asking questions and bumping into each other to get near the window. Jessica pressed against the glass for a better look.

"I don't see it anymore," she said to Elizabeth.

"Me, neither," Elizabeth said in a disappointed voice.

Just then, the lights came back on. Jessica blinked and looked around.

"OK," Jennifer said. "Quit joking about seeing the ghost."

"We really saw something!" Winston said. "It looked like the ghost."

"You saw a person," Jennifer laughed. "A person wearing a raincoat with a hood. That's not very ghostly."

Jessica tried to remember what she had seen. It had looked like a person. But it wasn't dressed like anybody she had ever seen before.

"Look," Elizabeth said, pointing at a picture on the wall. "We saw somebody dressed like that."

The campers crowded around to see. The picture was of six men in long, brown robes with hoods. They had ropes tied around their waists instead of belts, and they wore sandals.

"Those were the monks of San Benito," Mr. Sanchez said. He looked puzzled. "You saw someone dressed like that?"

"I'm getting goose bumps," Lila said.

"It was probably just someone in a poncho," Mr. Sanchez said. "That's all. I think you kids can go back to camp now. I hope you enjoyed your ghost story and I hope you all come back and visit the museum again."

Jessica looked at the other Snoopers. Her eyes were shining with excitement. "This sure is a mystery," she said quietly, so none of the other campers would hear.

"We could make this our next case," Eva whispered.

"Yeah," Winston said. "The mystery of the monk's ghost."

"We can find out if the ghost is real," Elizabeth said.

Jessica was so excited that she couldn't stop smiling. Day camp was becoming more fun by the minute.

CHAPTER 4

A Strange Message

When the group went outside, the rain had stopped, and the sky was beginning to show between the clouds again. "The storm's over," Jennifer said. "Let's go back."

Their feet went *squish-squish* in the wet grass. Jessica walked on her tiptoes to keep her sneakers dry.

"What should we do first?" Todd asked the other Snoopers.

"First," Amy said, "we need some clues."

Elizabeth put her hands in her pockets and walked along quietly. She didn't really believe in ghosts, but she wasn't completely sure.

Mrs. Bramson, the camp director, was waiting for them. "My goodness!" she said. "I thought you all got washed away."

"We went to the San Benito Museum," Jessica said. "And we saw a ghost!"

"We did," Eva said. "The monk's ghost."

Mrs. Bramson looked surprised. "Not a real ghost."

Elizabeth and the Snoopers looked at each other. They didn't know if it was real or not, but they were going to try to find out.

While the Porpoises told Mrs. Bramson about the museum, another counselor asked her for the key to the arts and crafts room. Mrs. Bramson gave it to him, and then asked for quiet.

"OK, let's settle down," she said firmly. "You—"

"Mrs. Bramson!" came a yell from the supply room.

Everyone froze for an instant. Then Mrs. Bramson began running toward the supply room.

"Come on," Todd said to the Snoopers. They ran after the director, and the other kids followed with Jennifer.

When they got to the small storage room, they crowded around to see what had happened. Elizabeth looked in and felt her stomach do a somersault.

The room looked like a tornado had gone through it. Paper was scattered everywhere. Crayons and pencils had been dumped onto the floor, and paint was spilled over everything. On the wall opposite the door were two words written in orange paint: GO AWAY!

"Oh, my gosh!" Winston gasped.

"What does it mean?" Lila asked.

25

Mrs. Bramson was standing in the middle of the room. She kept shaking her head. "Who would do a thing like this?" she asked sadly.

"It was the ghost!" Sandy Ferris yelled.

Elizabeth looked over her shoulder. Everyone was starting to whisper about the ghost.

"It wasn't a ghost." Mrs. Bramson said quickly. "Don't be silly."

The Snoopers huddled in a corner and kept their voices down. "Mrs. Bramson has the only key to this room," Todd whispered. "She usually keeps it in her pocket."

"Or in her office," Elizabeth said.

"So nobody could get in," Jessica said. "This room is always locked."

They stared at each other. "A *ghost* could get in," Ellen said. "Ghosts don't need keys."

"What's all the fuss?" asked a loud voice.

Joe Larson, the camp cook, was standing

nearby. He wiped his hands on a dish towel and looked over the campers' heads.

"A ghost got in and wrecked the art supplies," Ricky Capaldo told him. "The ghost from San Benito!"

"And we saw it," Andy Franklin said.

Joe whistled. "Really? I heard there was a ghost."

"It's real, too," Ricky said.

"I hope it keeps away from me," Joe said with a laugh.

"Now, Joe," Mrs. Bramson said. "Don't encourage them."

Joe shrugged. "I'll clean this up, Mrs. B.," he said.

"Come on, everyone," Jennifer said. "Let's go outside."

One by one, the campers filed out. The Snoopers walked out to the front steps and sat down.

"Who do you think did it, Elizabeth?" Todd asked.

Elizabeth put her arms around her knees. "I don't know," she said slowly.

"I'll bet you anything it was the ghost," Winston said.

"I don't believe in ghosts," Ellen said.

"Then how come you look so scared?" Lila asked her.

"I believe in ghosts," Eva said. "I knew this girl once who saw a shape—"

"Don't tell me," Jessica said, putting her hands on her ears. "I don't want to hear anything scary."

Elizabeth looked across the sports field at the wall. She could see the very top of the bell tower.

Was the ghost real, after all?

CHAPTER 5

The First Clue

Jessica sat down at the dinner table and took a deep breath. "Guess what we saw at day camp today?" she said.

"What, honey?" Mrs. Wakefield asked.

"Aliens from outer space?" Steven said. Steven was the twins' older brother. He was nine, and he loved to tease them. "With green skin and hairy teeth?"

"That's so funny I forgot to laugh," Jessica said. She took a sip of her milk. "We saw a ghost at San Benito Museum. And then it wrecked the art supplies."

Mr. Wakefield smiled as he helped himself to some salad. "Is that right?" he said in a teasing voice.

"We saw something," Elizabeth explained. "It looked like a monk. And the art supplies really were messed up—"

"And the ghost painted 'GO AWAY' on the wall," Jessica added.

"I think that's terrible," Mrs. Wakefield said, sounding angry. "It must be someone's idea of a cruel joke."

Jessica shook her head. "It could have been a ghost, you know."

"A ghost! Oh, no! It's going to get me!" Steven pretended to be scared. He shivered and made his teeth chatter.

"Well, someone did it," Elizabeth said.

Jessica looked at her sister. Someone did it, she thought, and the Snoopers were going to find out who.

The next morning, the Snoopers had planned to have a secret meeting before camp began. After everyone's parents dropped them off, they went behind the dining room. They could hear Joe banging pots and pans around inside the kitchen.

"Sandy Ferris's mother called my mother last night," Ellen told everyone. "She said she's not letting Sandy go to a camp where so many strange things are going on."

"We always give Lois Waller a ride to camp," Eva said. "But her mother didn't let her come today."

Jessica kicked a crumpled piece of aluminum foil toward the garbage can. "Our mother thinks it's a mean joke that someone is playing."

"I heard Mrs. Bramson talking on the phone when I got here," Todd added. "She was saying that nothing like that would happen again."

Winston shrugged. "She doesn't know for sure. The ghost could come back any time it wants to."

"If it *is* a ghost," Elizabeth said.

Everyone was quiet. Winston shrugged and looked down at the ground. "Hey, look at this," he said suddenly. "Orange paint."

"That's the same kind of paint that 'GO AWAY' was written with," Jessica said in an excited voice.

There were drops of orange paint on the ground near the garbage can. Todd took the lid off the can and looked inside. "Here's a rag with more paint on it."

Amy carefully unfolded the rag. There were smears of orange paint all over it.

"Somebody wiped their hands on that," Lila said.

Eva giggled. "Ghosts don't need to wipe their hands," she pointed out.

"So it must have been a real person who wrote the 'GO AWAY' message," Elizabeth said.

Jessica took a closer look at the paint rag. Then she made a face. "That's the same kind of paint I was using yesterday on my clay pot."

Nobody said anything. They all looked at the orange paint marks.

"It could be the same paint," Todd said. "Jessica could have used it, and then the person who wrote the sign could have used it."

"Or it could still be a ghost that did it," Ellen whispered. She gulped.

Jessica took a step closer to her sister. Talking about ghosts was beginning to make her very nervous.

Todd put the rag back in the garbage can.

"Remember what Mr. Sanchez said about the ghost? Seeing the ghost means trouble is coming."

"No," Elizabeth said quickly. "That's only if the bells in the bell tower ring."

"Yeah, but the bells don't work anymore," Lila said. "So maybe the ghost can't ring them to warn us, and he had to write the sign. The ghost was telling us to go away because there was danger."

Suddenly, all the Snoopers became very quiet. The mystery was getting more mysterious by the minute.

CHAPTER 6

More Clues

Elizabeth climbed up the ladder of the swimming pool. The Porpoises had almost finished their morning swim. The eight-year-old group, the Dolphins, was next. Elizabeth and Jessica stood together at the side of the pool. Jessica drew wet circles on the cement with her toe.

"I need two helpers," Jennifer said as she walked over to the twins. "Can you take our attendance sheet to Mrs. Bramson's office for me?"

"OK," Elizabeth said, taking the sheet.

The twins put on their sneakers. Jessica wrapped her towel around her shoulders and walked ahead. "This is my fur cape," she said. "Don't I look like a movie star?"

"No," Elizabeth said, giggling. They went inside and down the hall to Mrs. Bramson's office. Elizabeth started to knock on the door, but she heard a loud, angry voice.

"I've said no and I mean no!" the voice said.

"That's Mrs. Bramson," Jessica whispered. Her eyes widened. "It sounds like someone's getting in trouble."

Elizabeth felt embarrassed. She hated to hear anyone get scolded. But then they heard a man's voice.

"Mrs. Bramson, let's be reasonable," he said. "I can give you a good price for this camp."

"Camp San Benito has been in my family

38

for forty years," Mrs. Bramson said. "I'm not going to sell it."

Jessica gulped and stared at Elizabeth. "Should we knock?" she asked very quietly.

"Umm . . ." Elizabeth knew they shouldn't stand in the hall and listen. They had to hand in the attendance sheet, but she didn't want to interrupt.

"She sounds really angry at that man," Jessica added.

"Let's just push it under the door," Elizabeth said. She bent down and slid the paper through the space at the bottom. Then they turned and began tiptoeing away.

Suddenly they heard the door open. "Hurry," Jessica said.

"I'll be back," the man said to Mrs. Bramson. His voice sounded even louder, since the door was open.

Elizabeth and Jessica could see the man

begin to walk down the hall toward them. Elizabeth was afraid he might think they had been spying on him. So she grabbed Jessica's hand and raced out the door.

"Thanks for running that errand," Jennifer said when the twins got back to the pool. "Now hurry up and change. It's time for lunch."

As Elizabeth changed out of her wet suit, she thought about Mrs. Bramson. She felt very sorry for her. Campers were staying away because of the story about the monk's ghost. And now a man was trying to buy the camp.

When they stood in the lunch line, Elizabeth could hear everyone talking about the ghost. No one knew if it was real or not. But everyone was very excited about it.

"Can I have an orange instead of an apple?" Elizabeth asked Joe when it was her turn.

Joe frowned. "There aren't any oranges. They're gone."

"What happened to them?" Jennifer asked.

"I'm not sure," Joe grumbled. "All I know is, I had four bags of oranges here this morning. I went outside for a minute, and when I came back, all four bags were gone."

"Somebody must have come in and taken them," Todd said.

Joe looked doubtful. "In *one* minute, while my back was turned, somebody took *four* whole bags?"

"Maybe it was the ghost," Winston suggested.

"Why would the ghost want oranges?" Jessica asked.

"Some ghosts just like to make trouble," Lila said in her know-it-all way. "I saw that in a TV show."

Elizabeth looked at Joe. "Do you think it was a ghost?"

Instead of answering, Joe shrugged his shoulders. Then he put a peanut butter and jelly sandwich on Elizabeth's plate. "If you want to jump to conclusions . . ." he said slowly.

Everyone could hear what Joe was saying, and pretty soon the whole lunch line was buzzing.

"Come on, let's keep the line moving," Jennifer said.

Elizabeth picked up her tray and moved along. Why would a ghost steal oranges? It didn't make sense. But Elizabeth didn't know who else could have done it.

CHAPTER 7

Mysterious Footprints

The weather was so nice that Jennifer decided to let the Porpoises have their rest hour outside. She spread out some blankets on the grass. Jessica was between Elizabeth and Lila, and the rest of the Snoopers were nearby.

It was a clear, sunny day. A cool breeze rustled through the leaves. Jessica looked over at the bell tower of San Benito. The tower didn't seem one bit spooky anymore.

When rest hour was over, the campers stood up, stretched, and began to fold their blankets.

Then, a loud *DING DONG*! filled the air.

"That came from the bell tower," Lila gasped.

Everyone stared at the bell tower. One after another, bell tones rang out.

"But the bells are broken," Elizabeth said. "They don't have any metal ringers, remember?"

The Snoopers glanced at each other. Ellen looked pretty scared. Jessica felt a little scared, too.

"Come on," Todd said. He got up and started to run toward the bell tower.

Jessica didn't have time to think. She started running, too. The rest of the Snoopers were right behind her. The ringing stopped, but the Snoopers kept going.

"Kids!" Jennifer yelled. "Where are you going?"

Jessica kept running along with the others. She wanted to find out how the bells could have been ringing.

The Snoopers ran through the gate of San Benito. Mr. Sanchez was standing in the courtyard, staring up at the bell tower. Jessica noticed that he looked very surprised when they all raced by.

Elizabeth and Todd opened the door and started to race up the stairs. Jessica was right behind them. She could hear the others following.

Jessica was scared, nervous, and excited all at once. Maybe they would solve the mystery right now. Their feet banged on the wooden steps, and Jessica felt dizzy from the twists and turns. Finally, they came to a door.

"We can open it on the count of three," Todd panted. "One, two—"

"Three!" Elizabeth said. They pushed the door open.

In front of them was a bright, airy room. The bells hung from the ceiling. A thick layer of dust covered the floor.

"Look," Eva said, pointing to the floor. "Footprints."

The Snoopers all crowded into the doorway. Jessica could see that the footprints led from the door to the corner and back to the door again.

"Can ghosts leave footprints?" Winston asked.

"No, silly," Lila said. "Everybody knows that."

"Well, maybe some ghosts do," Ellen said nervously.

Jessica leaned into the room and looked up inside the bells. They were empty. There

were no ringers inside to hit against the sides and make them ring.

"But how did they ring?" she asked.

Nobody knew the answer.

"What are you kids doing?" Jennifer panted as she reached the top of the stairs. She looked angry and upset. "Why on earth did you run off like that?"

Mr. Sanchez came up behind her. "What's going on?"

"We're trying to solve the mystery," Elizabeth said.

"What mystery?" Mr. Sanchez asked.

"Of the monk's ghost," Amy said. "We want to find out if it's real, and if it's haunting the camp."

Jennifer's mouth dropped open. "That's silly—"

"Somebody's doing something!" Todd said. "We want to find out who."

The counselor looked at them and shook her head slowly. "I think you should leave that to us," she said.

Jessica looked at her sister. They weren't going to leave things to the grown-ups. They were going to find out for themselves.

CHAPTER 8

The Snoopers' Big Plan

When they got back to camp, the Snoopers had to apologize to Mrs. Bramson. Elizabeth felt very sorry about running away. But they had to solve the mystery.

At four-thirty, everyone stood out front to wait for their parents to pick them up to go home.

"You know what we should do?" Todd said. "We should watch the bell tower. We could do it after camp, when no one knows we're here."

Elizabeth felt a shiver go up her back. She

still wasn't sure if she believed in ghosts, but she certainly felt nervous now.

"Not me," Lila said. "I'm not going there at night."

"We wouldn't be allowed to anyway," Amy reminded them.

Jessica played with the Velcro on her sneakers. Elizabeth could tell that her sister was nervous. Twins could always tell.

"I would be afraid," Eva said honestly. "In the dark."

"Hey," Elizabeth said. She looked at the other campers nearby and lowered her voice. "The camp-out is this weekend, on the sports field. We could watch the tower then."

"Yeah. It's called a stake-out. We could take turns watching the tower," Winston said. "Then if anything happens, one of us will see it."

Ellen was shaking her head. "I heard Mrs.

Bramson say she might cancel the camp-out," she told them, "because so many kids are afraid of the ghost."

Elizabeth felt disappointed. "She can't! I'm not scared to camp out. We did it in our backyard. Right, Jess?"

Jessica nodded. She remembered the time she and Elizabeth, Amy, Lila, Ellen, and Eva had slept outside in a tent in their backyard.

"Let's go see Mrs. Bramson," Todd said.

They all stood up together and trooped into Mrs. Bramson's office. "Hello, kids. What can I do for you?" she asked.

"We don't want you to cancel the camp-out," Elizabeth said.

Mrs. Bramson looked at each of them. "Well, I was considering it."

"But we really, really, really want to have it," Jessica blurted out. "Please don't cancel it."

"That was going to be the best part of camp," Winston added. "I'm getting a new sleeping bag just for it."

"You kids aren't scared?" Mrs. Bramson asked.

"No," Elizabeth and Todd said quickly. Elizabeth looked at Jessica, and Jessica nodded.

"I'm not *really* scared," Eva said quietly.

"Well . . ." Mrs. Bramson picked up a pencil and tapped it on her desk. "Maybe we should do it after all. It would be a shame if I spoiled your fun because of a few scaredy-cats."

Elizabeth breathed a sigh of relief. "So you won't cancel it?"

"No. I think you're right." Mrs. Bramson stood up and gave them all a big smile. "Not everyone will be coming, but that doesn't mean we can't have fun."

"Goody, goody, goody!" Jessica said as the Snoopers left the office. "I can't wait."

"I can," Ellen said. She looked at the others. "But I'm a Snooper, so I'll go, too."

"Let's shake on it," Todd suggested.

He put his hand out and made a fist. Elizabeth made a fist, too, and tapped Todd on the knuckles. Everyone else gave each other the secret Snoopers handshake.

The Snoopers were going to stake out San Benito.

The next morning, Elizabeth ran down to breakfast early.

"We're having waffles today," Mrs. Wakefield said.

"Yum!" Steven shouted. "I want six."

"Make it two," Mr. Wakefield said with a laugh. "I don't want to have to keep you home with a stomachache." He opened the newspaper and began to read.

Jessica walked into the kitchen, still in her pajamas, and yawned. She always felt sleepy first thing in the morning.

"Hey, look at this," Mr. Wakefield said. He sounded surprised. "Here's an article about your day camp."

Elizabeth stood up and looked over her father's shoulder. There was a picture of the main building of Camp San Benito and another of the bell tower.

"The headline says 'Ghostly Events at Local Camp,'" Elizabeth read.

Mr. Wakefield was reading the article quickly. He looked very serious. "The article is about some strange happenings, and it mentions the ghost story you all heard. It seems a lot of parents are taking their kids out of camp."

"Oh, really?" Mrs. Wakefield asked as she sat down next to him and scanned the article. "I didn't know it was so serious."

Elizabeth and Jessica looked at each other. Their mother sounded very concerned.

"But, Mom," Elizabeth said quickly. "We're not scared."

"I don't like this," Mrs. Wakefield said with a frown on her face. "Maybe you girls shouldn't—"

"Oh, Mom!" Jessica interrupted. She shook her head. "We really like camp. Don't make us leave. Please."

Elizabeth crossed her fingers. She loved camp. Besides, if their mother didn't let them go back, the Snoopers wouldn't be able to solve the mystery.

"Something like this could be very bad for business," Mr. Wakefield said. "If people think it's not a good camp, Mrs. Bramson could be ruined."

Elizabeth stared at her father. "You mean, she would have to close the whole camp down?"

"Yes, I'm afraid that's true," Mr. Wakefield said. "If nobody wants to go there, then the camp might close."

Elizabeth gave her sister a worried look. Now it was more important than ever to solve the mystery. If the Snoopers found out what was going on, then other campers wouldn't be afraid and their parents wouldn't take them out of camp.

They had to do something.

CHAPTER 9
The Stake-Out

Friday night was the camp-out. Joe set up a big grill in the sports field. "Hot dogs, burgers, and then marshmallows for dessert," he said. "The perfect dinner."

"And we don't have to eat any vegetables if we don't want to," Jessica said happily. "Right?"

Joe smiled at her. "Not on a camp-out."

The Snoopers were excited and nervous about their stake-out. They didn't want anybody else to know about it, though.

"I can't wait for it to get dark," Todd said,

biting into a hot dog. "I hope the ghost comes out tonight."

"I don't," Ellen said. "I hope I'm asleep then."

Jessica stood up. "I'm getting another soda."

"Me, too," Elizabeth said.

The twins walked over to the picnic table. Mrs. Bramson and Jennifer and the other counselors were there. "Can we have some more soda?" Elizabeth asked, holding out her cup.

Jennifer picked up a can and shook it. "Empty."

"There's plenty more in the kitchen," Mrs. Bramson said. "Would you two like to bring some out?"

"Sure," Jessica said.

The two girls walked to the back door of the kitchen and walked inside. They saw a man there, with his back to them. He turned around in surprise and quickly put something in a paper bag.

"Hey, hey," he said. "You startled me."

"We're sorry," Elizabeth said. "We just came to get more soda."

"What are you doing?" Jessica asked. She felt curious about what he was doing there. He looked a little bit familiar.

The man seemed nervous. "You can keep a secret, can't you?"

Jessica loved secrets. But she could tell her sister didn't like the man at all.

"I'm a friend of Mrs. Bramson's," the man said with a smile. "But don't tell her I'm here, OK? I want it to be a surprise."

"OK," Jessica said. Elizabeth didn't say anything.

"I know I can count on you." The man took his paper bag and walked out quickly.

"I wonder why he doesn't want Mrs. Bramson to know he was here," Jessica said.

Elizabeth opened the big refrigerator and took out two bottles of soda. "You know what? That was the same man we saw outside of Mrs. Bramson's office. He was the one who was arguing with her."

"You're right!" Jessica gasped. "They aren't friends at all." She frowned. "Why would he lie to us?"

"What was that thing he put into the bag?" Elizabeth asked.

Jessica squeezed her eyes shut. She tried to remember what it had looked like. "I think it was a tape recorder."

"That's funny," Elizabeth said. "Let's go back outside."

They went back to the field and gave the soda bottles to the counselors. Then they went over and sat with their friends. They quickly told the other Snoopers about the mysterious man. "Let's list all our clues," Elizabeth said.

"Good idea," Amy replied.

"Here comes Jennifer," Jessica said.

"Hey, everyone," their counselor said. "What's up?"

All the Snoopers looked at each other. Elizabeth raised her eyebrows. "Should we tell her?"

"Yes," Todd agreed. The others nodded.

Jennifer's eyes widened. "You're all being very mysterious."

"Well, we have a mystery to solve," Jessica said. "The mystery of the monk's ghost."

Jennifer was smiling. But when she saw how serious they were, she looked serious, too. "OK. Fill me in."

"First, we saw someone who was dressed like a monk during the rainstorm," Eliza-

64

beth said. "Then someone got into the arts and crafts supply room and wrote on the walls and wrecked the room. Someone who could get a key—"

"Or who doesn't need a key," Ellen cut in.

Jennifer frowned. "Well, if it's a real person, the person had to get the key. That tells me it could be someone who works here at the camp."

"That's right," Elizabeth said. Her eyes were shining.

"Then the bells rang, even though they can't," Amy said.

"I'll bet you could make them ring with a hammer," Todd said.

"Next we saw footprints in the bell tower," Jessica reminded them. "That has to have been a real person."

"Or a ghost who can leave footprints," Ellen said.

"A ghost can't leave footprints," Elizabeth said.

Jennifer thought for a moment. "It sounds like a person is trying to make us *think* there's a ghost," she said.

"But why?" Eva asked.

The Snoopers shook their heads in puzzlement.

That was what they couldn't figure out.

CHAPTER 10

The Camp Fire Ghost

"It's time for the camp fire," Mrs. Bramson called out when it was dark. "Everybody gather around. It's marshmallow time!"

Elizabeth finished spreading out her sleeping bag next to Jessica's. Then she jumped up and ran over to the camp fire Joe had built. Everyone was sitting around it. Elizabeth squeezed in between Jennifer and Eva.

Jennifer showed everyone how to put a marshmallow on the end of a twig and toast it over the fire.

"This is really fun," Jessica said happily. "I'm glad our camp-out didn't get canceled."

"Me, too," Jennifer said. She looked around at the group. Only about half of the kids from camp were there. "We've got sort of a skeleton crew."

Elizabeth giggled. "Don't say that," she said. "You'll scare everyone."

"I wouldn't be afraid of any old ghost if it came," Charlie Cashman said.

"Me, neither," Winston said. "I'd go up to it and—"

"And scare it back," Lila said.

Elizabeth sat with her legs crossed and stared at the fire. It was fun to be outside at night, wondering if the ghost would come. The darker it got, the more she wondered if there really could be a ghost.

"You know what I would do if a ghost came," Ron Reese bragged. "I'd punch it in the nose."

"I dare you to walk out into the field where it's dark," Ellen said.

Ron put his chin in the air and laughed. But he didn't move an inch.

"What if the ghost is real?" Jessica whispered. "We could be wrong about all those clues, you know."

"I know," Elizabeth agreed.

"When should we start taking turns watching the tower?" Eva asked.

Elizabeth gulped. "I—I'm not sure."

"I hope nothing happens during my turn," Amy said.

It was very quiet. Everyone stared into the fire.

Suddenly, Jessica jumped to her feet. "Look, everyone," she shouted, pointing to the dark field.

Everyone turned to look. A figure in a hooded robe was walking toward the fire.

Jessica and Lila screamed. Elizabeth dropped her marshmallow.

"The ghost!" Winston shouted.

"Stop right there!" Mrs. Bramson commanded.

She switched on her flashlight and shone it on the ghost. In the light, everyone could see it was Robert Marcy, one of the campers. He was wearing a bathrobe with a hood. He started laughing.

"That's not funny," Lila said angrily.

"Robert, take that robe off right now," Jennifer said. Her voice sounded angry, but she was smiling.

Elizabeth realized how scared everyone had been. Then she started giggling. Pretty soon, everyone else was laughing, too.

"Good joke," Todd said. He punched Robert in the arm.

"You guys were terrified," Robert laughed. "What a bunch of chickens."

"I'll bet there really isn't any ghost," Amy said to the other Snoopers. "It's silly to believe in them, anyway."

Winston nodded. "Yeah, you're right. Ghosts are just make believe."

"OK, kids. Settle down. There's nothing to be scared of. Look at the bell tower," Jennifer said. "I mean, does that look scary? I think it looks pretty at night."

Elizabeth looked at the museum. The tower was outlined in the moonlight. It looked pretty and peaceful. There was nothing at all to be afraid of, she decided.

"Let's have our sing-along," Mrs. Bramson suggested. "Who knows 'The Elephant in My Room'?"

She started singing the song, and pretty soon, all the campers joined in. Elizabeth rocked back and forth to bump shoulders with Eva and Jennifer. She was having fun.

Some of the boys got up and pretended to be elephants. Elizabeth started laughing so hard she could barely sing. Then she heard a sound. She stopped singing and tried to listen. "The bells!" she whispered.

One by one, the singers stopped. The bells of San Benito were ringing out in the darkness.

"Oh, no," Jessica said.

All the campers turned and looked at the bell tower. While they watched, a ghostly figure appeared on the roof. Then it seemed to disappear.

"The ghost! That's him for real!" Robert yelled.

Several campers jumped up and started screaming. Mrs. Bramson stood up and headed for the office. "This is the last straw," she announced. "I'm calling the police!"

73

CHAPTER 11

Ghost Catchers

"**I**'m going to check this out," Jennifer said to Peter, one of the Dolphin's counselors. She picked up a flashlight, and they started running toward San Benito.

Jessica looked at the other Snoopers. They had run away from camp once already. And they knew it was wrong. But this time, they might be able to catch the ghost.

"Come on," Todd said. He and Elizabeth started running after Jennifer and Peter. The rest of the Snoopers chased after them, too.

"We should split up," Elizabeth yelled over

her shoulder. "We'll make sure he doesn't get away!"

Jessica knew she wanted to stick with her sister. Eva, Todd, Winston, and Amy veered off to the left. Jessica, Elizabeth, Ellen, and Lila ran through the gate of the museum.

"He was up there," Jennifer called out up ahead. The Snoopers could see her running toward the stairs leading to the bell tower.

The bells were still ringing. The courtyard was empty, and they could barely see the fountain in the dark. Jessica stopped to catch her breath.

"Come on," Elizabeth said, dashing back to her.

"I'm coming." Jessica started running again.

"There he is!" Elizabeth pointed to a shadowy archway.

Jessica glimpsed the ghostly figure in the

hooded robe. The figure stopped for a moment and then began to run.

"Cut him off!" Jennifer yelled.

Jessica ran faster than she had ever run in her life. She was scared. But she wanted to solve the mystery, too.

The ghostly figure was ahead of them. He kept dodging around pillars and archways. Then he tripped on his long robe and stumbled.

"Get him!" Elizabeth gasped.

At the same time, all the Snoopers and Jennifer dove on the ghost. Jessica grabbed a foot and hung on. It was a person's foot—not a ghost's. She was sure of that.

Jennifer turned on her flashlight and pointed it in the intruder's face.

"Joe!" they all shouted.

Police sirens started wailing in the distance.

"Let go of me, you crazy kids," Joe mut-

tered. He tried to stand up, but Ellen and Lila sat on his chest. Jessica hung onto his foot and didn't let go.

"Why did you do it?" Jessica asked.

Joe stopped struggling. He shook his head and didn't answer.

They could hear the police sirens stop outside the museum. Elizabeth and Jessica stood up. "We'll bring them here," Elizabeth said.

The twins ran out to the main courtyard. Peter and the other Snoopers were there. Standing between them was the man the twins had seen in the kitchen.

"He had a tape recorder of ringing bells," Winston told them excitedly.

"And we just caught Joe," Elizabeth announced.

"HOLD IT RIGHT THERE!" boomed a voice on a megaphone.

The Snoopers froze where they were.

CHAPTER 12

The Snoopers
Save the Day

Two police officers ran into the courtyard. "What's going on here?" one of them asked.

Everyone started talking at once. The officer put two fingers in his mouth and whistled loudly. "OK, OK, one at a time," he said. "Who's in charge of these kids?"

Jennifer stepped forward. "I am. But I'm not sure I can really explain things very well."

"Excuse me," Elizabeth said. She raised her hand.

"Yes, young lady?" the second officer asked.

"I think I can explain," Elizabeth said. "Joe is the cook at Camp San Benito. He and that man want to close down the camp by making everyone think it's haunted."

The first officer took out a notebook and pencil. "Go on."

"They played a tape recording of bells," Todd said.

"And made it seem like a ghost was doing bad things at camp," Jessica added.

Elizabeth looked at Joe. He was still wearing the monk's robe, but he was staring at the ground. The other man had his arms folded.

"And just why would they do a thing like that?" the second officer asked.

Elizabeth bit her lip. She was still trying to figure it all out. "I think it's because that man wants to buy the camp, and Mrs. Bramson won't sell it to him."

"How did you—" Joe's friend blurted out.

"We heard him arguing with Mrs. Bramson," Jessica said.

"So, you wanted to buy, and you got the cook to help you out, huh?" the first officer said to Joe's friend. "Land is getting pretty valuable around here and you thought you could get a good price."

"I knew it was an inside job," Todd said, sounding just like a detective from the movies.

The police officers put handcuffs on the two criminals. "You two are coming to the station with us," the second officer said.

Joe stared at the Snoopers. "You had to go sticking your noses in, didn't you?"

Elizabeth stared back at him. Part of her was glad to solve the mystery. Now they knew there was no ghost. But she was sorry that Joe was a criminal.

"Come on, you super snoops," Jennifer said. "It's time to get back to camp."

In the morning, the Snoopers found out the whole story. Joe's friend was named Evan. He had told the police everything. It was exactly the way the Snoopers had figured it out. Joe had messed up the arts and crafts supply room, and he had made up the story about the stolen oranges.

"We solved the mystery," Elizabeth told her parents proudly when they came to pick up the twins.

Mr. and Mrs. Wakefield looked very happy. "My goodness," Mrs. Wakefield said. "It looks like you saved Camp San Benito."

"Now everyone can come back to camp," Jennifer said happily.

"Here are my heroes," Mrs. Bramson said as she walked up. "There's a photographer here from the newspaper. You're going to be famous."

Jessica's mouth dropped open. "We're getting our pictures in the paper?"

"That's right. We have to go to the bell tower now," Mrs. Bramson said. "Mr. Sanchez is waiting for us."

Elizabeth grinned. They were going to be in the paper. They were going to be famous detectives.

Everyone trooped over to the museum, and Mr. Sanchez took them to the bell tower. The photographer had bags and cameras hanging from his shoulders.

When Mr. Sanchez opened the door to the bell room, Elizabeth stepped inside first. The large bells hung from the ceiling. She could see in all directions through the big windows.

"It's so pretty up here," she said. "I can almost see my house."

"Too nice for ghosts," Jennifer agreed.

Winston folded his arms. "I never believed it was a real ghost," he said.

"Me, neither," Todd said quickly.

"Me, neither," Ellen agreed.

The rest of the Snoopers stared at her. Ellen turned pink. "Well . . ." she mumbled.

"The legend of the monk's ghost is just a legend," Mr. Sanchez said gently. "That's all it is. There's no ghost."

"I know," Jessica said. She turned around underneath a bell. "But from now on, every time I hear a bell ringing I'm going to get goose bumps."

Everyone laughed. The photographer had the Snoopers line up against the wall. Elizabeth looked at Jennifer and smiled. "You have to be in it, too," she said.

Jennifer shook her head. "You solved the mystery yourselves and caught the fake ghosts. I didn't do anything."

After the photographer took the pictures, Mrs. Bramson made an announcement.

"As a special reward, we're going to have another camp-out. And this time, I hope we won't have any interruptions from ghosts or criminals," she said.

Jessica grinned. "I love day camp."

Elizabeth giggled. That wasn't what Jessica had said before they had a mystery to solve. She looked at the Snoopers and smiled. She couldn't wait to start their next case.

SWEET VALLEY KIDS

Jessica and Elizabeth have had lots of adventures in *Sweet Valley High* and *Sweet Valley Twins*...now read about the twins at age seven! You'll love all the fun that comes with being seven—birthday parties, playing dress-up, class projects, putting on puppet shows and plays, losing a tooth, setting up lemonade stands, caring for animals and much more! It's all part of SWEET VALLEY KIDS. Read them all!

☐	SURPRISE! SURPRISE! #1	15758-2	$2.99/$3.50
☐	RUNAWAY HAMSTER #2	15759-0	$2.99/$3.50
☐	THE TWINS' MYSTERY TEACHER # 3	15760-4	$2.99/$3.50
☐	ELIZABETH'S VALENTINE # 4	15761-2	$2.99/$3.50
☐	JESSICA'S CAT TRICK # 5	15768-X	$2.99/$3.50
☐	LILA'S SECRET # 6	15773-6	$2.99/$3.50
☐	JESSICA'S BIG MISTAKE # 7	15799-X	$2.99/$3.50
☐	JESSICA'S ZOO ADVENTURE # 8	15802-3	$2.99/$3.50
☐	ELIZABETH'S SUPER-SELLING LEMONADE #9	15807-4	$2.99/$3.50
☐	THE TWINS AND THE WILD WEST #10	15811-2	$2.99/$3.50
☐	CRYBABY LOIS #11	15818-X	$2.99/$3.50
☐	SWEET VALLEY TRICK OR TREAT #12	15825-2	$2.75/$3.25
☐	STARRING WINSTON EGBERT #13	15836-8	$2.99/$3.50
☐	JESSICA THE BABY-SITTER #14	15838-4	$2.99/$3.50
☐	FEARLESS ELIZABETH #15	15844-9	$2.99/$3.50
☐	JESSICA THE TV STAR #16	15850-3	$2.75/$3.25
☐	CAROLINE'S MYSTERY DOLLS #17	15870-8	$2.99/$3.50
☐	BOSSY STEVEN #18	15881-3	$2.99/$3.50
☐	JESSICA AND THE JUMBO FISH #19	15936-4	$2.99/$3.50
☐	THE TWINS GO TO THE HOSPITAL #20	15912-7	$2.99/$3.50
☐	THE CASE OF THE SECRET SANTA (SVK Super Snooper #1)	15860-0	$2.95/$3.50
☐	THE CASE OF THE MAGIC CHRISTMAS BELL (SVK Super Snooper #2)	15964-X	$2.99/$3.50
☐	THE CASE OF THE HAUNTED DAY CAMP (SVK Super Snooper #3)	15894-5	$3.25/$3.99
☐	THE CASE OF THE CHRISTMAS THIEF (SVK Super Snooper #4)	48063-4	$3.25/$3.99

SWEET VALLEY KIDS

Jessica and Elizabeth have had lots of adventures in *Sweet Valley High* and *Sweet Valley Twins*...now read about the twins at age seven! You'll love all the fun that comes with being seven—birthday parties, playing dress-up, class projects, putting on puppet shows and plays, losing a tooth, setting up lemonade stands, caring for animals and much more! It's all part of SWEET VALLEY KIDS. Read them all!

☐ JESSICA AND THE SPELLING-BEE SURPRISE #21	15917-8	$2.75
☐ SWEET VALLEY SLUMBER PARTY #22	15934-8	$2.99
☐ LILA'S HAUNTED HOUSE PARTY # 23	15919-4	$2.99
☐ COUSIN KELLY'S FAMILY SECRET # 24	15920-8	$2.99
☐ LEFT-OUT ELIZABETH # 25	15921-6	$2.99
☐ JESSICA'S SNOBBY CLUB # 26	15922-4	$2.99
☐ THE SWEET VALLEY CLEANUP TEAM # 27	15923-2	$2.99
☐ ELIZABETH MEETS HER HERO #28	15924-0	$2.99
☐ ANDY AND THE ALIEN # 29	15925-9	$2.99
☐ JESSICA'S UNBURIED TREASURE # 30	15926-7	$2.99
☐ ELIZABETH AND JESSICA RUN AWAY # 31	48004-9	$2.99
☐ LEFT BACK! #32	48005-7	$2.99
☐ CAROLINE'S HALLOWEEN SPELL # 33	48006-5	$2.99
☐ THE BEST THANKSGIVING EVER # 34	48007-3	$2.99
☐ ELIZABETH'S BROKEN ARM # 35	48009-X	$2.99
☐ ELIZABETH'S VIDEO FEVER # 36	48010-3	$2.99
☐ THE BIG RACE # 37	48011-1	$2.99
☐ GOODBYE, EVA? # 38	48012-X	$2.99
☐ ELLEN IS HOME ALONE # 39	48013-8	$2.99